John Holmes

A Letter of Directions to his Father's Birthplace

John Holmes

A Letter of Directions to his Father's Birthplace

ISBN/EAN: 9783337048266

Printed in Europe, USA, Canada, Australia, Japan

Cover: Foto ©Raphael Reischuk / pixelio.de

More available books at **www.hansebooks.com**

A

LETTER OF DIRECTIONS

TO HIS

FATHER'S BIRTHPLACE,

BY

JOHN HOLMES.

WITH

NOTES AND A GENEALOGY BY D. WILLIAMS PATTERSON.

NEW YORK:

PRINTED FOR THE U. Q. CLUB.

1 8 6 5 .

Edition 99 copies 8vo.

42 " 4to. and

100 " 8vo. for the family.

SUBSCRIBERS' COPY.

No. 13

PRESS OF J. M. BRADSTREET & SON.

TO

Miss Frances Manwaring Caulkins,

THE ACCOMPLISHED HISTORIAN

OF THE TOWNS OF

NORWICH AND NEW LONDON,

· IN CONNECTICUT,

THE FOLLOWING PAGES ARE

MOST RESPECTFULLY INSCRIBED

BY

AN HUMBLE LABORER

IN A

NEIGHBORING FIELD.

WHAT FOR?

In arranging the *Folks Records of Eaſt Haddam, Conn.*, I tranſcribed from the *New England Hiſtorical and Genealogical Regiſter* Vol. X. p. 242, the *Letter of Directions* of John Holmes, wiſhing that ſome parts of it were clearer, but not doubting its correctneſs as a copy.

On the 15th of April laſt, through the kindneſs of Mr. Timothy Holmes, and his ſon, Silas R. Holmes, both of Hadlyme, in Eaſt Haddam, Conn., I was put in poſſeſſion of the original *Letter of Directions*, with a manuſcript copy of it, intended to aſſiſt thoſe who could not read the original.

On ſhowing this to ſome friends and pointing out the variations between the original and that copy in the *Regiſter*, I was urged to prepare an exact tranſcript, with notes, and append to it ſuch facts reſpecting the deſcendants of Thomas Holmes, as I had already collected in manuſcript in the work before named. The reſult follows. ,

Weſt Winſted, Conn.,

May 21, 1864.

Letter of Directions.

 HIS Letter of Directions—— from John Holmes[1]—in Haddam—in New England[2]—for to find—the place where his Father[3]—was Born and—Brought vp In London[4]: He was Son to Thomas Holmes— Councler[5] of Grafe-in[6] Who Liued in Saint-Tandrs-parrich[7] in Holborn[8]—in the Rofon Crown Cort[9] in Grafen Lain[10] upper fite[11]—a Gainft Grafin walks[12]—His

2

Mother's Maden Name was Mary Thetford[13]. Grandfather was Slain in the Time
of the Seuel wars—att Oxford Sege[14]—
Our : Cort:of:arms are the 3 Spord Coks
fighting in a Golden feild[15]— My father
Came out of England in the Time of
the Grat plage[16]—and he thought to haue
gon Down in to Norfolk[17]—to a place
Caled Lyn[18] whare—we—had a Small
pece of Land[19]—one Edmond Beel[20]—
was Tennant and had been for many
years before but all places being garded
he Culd Not pafs[21]—whear upon he
Came for uirjaney[22]—thenking to have
Returned—in a fue years[23]—But it was

other ways ordered—for the Contry proued unhelthy to : him and he was poor and Low in the world—after a while he Recruted—and as It was ordred —Marred—in New york[24] To one Lucrefe Dodly—Dafter[25] to—Mr— Thomas Dodley[26]—of London who Keep[27] the tanes Cort[28]—in—Clare Streat[29] in Common Gardin[30] in London. She had Two—Brothers[31]—But She Died—a bout 6—and thirty year a Go[32]—my father Died—in Dec^m 12th 1724[33]—Being a uery aged man[34]—my father fo long as he Liued he Liued in hopes of Seeing England a Gain—But he is Dead an

Gon and Left but only me his Son[86] being thirty—8—years—of age[86]   -   -   .

These Directions Taken by John Holmes on his father's Death bead[87].

NOTES.

Note 1. The surname HOLM, or HOLMES, is classed by Lower among those local names "which describe *the nature or situation of the original bearer's residence,* such as *Hill, Dale, Wood.*" He defines it as follows; " *Holm, Holmes,* flat land, a meadow surrounded with water; other islands, like those in the Bristol Channel."

English Surnames, third edition, vol. i., p. 74.

" HOLMES—a holme is defined by Halliwell as 'flatland; a small island; a deposite of soil at the confluence of two waters. Flat grounds near water are called holms.'"

"'Some call them the *holmes,* because they lie low, and are good for nothing but grasse'. *Harrison.*"

In Scotland a *holm* means both a small uninhabited island, and a detached or insulated rock in the sea."

Patronymica Britannica, p. 160.

Note 2. "Haddam, in New England," is a half-shire-town in Middlesex County, in the State of Connecticut, lying on the Connecticut River. It was originally called "The Plantation at Thirty Miles Island," and, including the present town of East Haddam, was bought of the Indians, May 20, 1662, for thirty coats, and was settled in the same year, by the twenty-eight proprietors, most of whom were from Hartford. The town was incorporated in October, 1668, by its present name. The original settlement was made on the west side of the river, but, as early as 1685, several families were living on the east side, and in October, 1700, were allowed by the Legislature to form a church on that side of the river, and to manage their ecclesiastical affairs by themselves.

Soon after this ecclesiastical division, the town voted to manage town affairs, and keep their records, separately, and, by consent of the Legislature, did so till 1734, when that part lying east of Connecticut and Salmon Rivers was incorporated as a town by the name of East Haddam. This had been commonly known as "Haddam on ye east side of ye great river." It was originally called Matchamoodus, Machamoodus, or Machimoodus, from the Indian words *matchit*—bad, or evil—and *moodus* —noises—, alluding to the subterranean noises and shakings which were formerly very frequent, and are still sometimes heard and felt, retaining the old name of "Moodus Noises." The village of Moodus derives its name from the old Indian name.

The first church in East Haddam was formed May 3, 1704, and Rev. Stephen Hosmer ordained as its pastor.

The second, or Millington Ecclesiastical Society was formed in October, 1733, and the church was organized Dec. 2, 1736, in the east part of the town.

The third, or Hadlyme Ecclesiastical Society was formed in November, 1742, and includes the south part of East Haddam, and the north-west part of Lyme, taking one syllable of its name from the name of each town. The church in Hadlyme was organized June 26, 1745.

The residence of Capt. John Holmes was in Hadlyme, about forty rods west of the Congregational
meeting-house. The place is still marked by a large
willow tree, and the foundation of the old chimney.

Note 3.   Mr. Holmes does not mention the Chris-
tian-name of his father, but the records show that it was
Thomas.   We first find him noticed in Connecticut, at
New London, in the record of the birth of his son John,
the writer of the *Letter of Directions*, March 11, 1686,
in reference to which date, Miss Frances M. Caulkins,
in answer to my enquiry, says: "I would observe that
March 11th, 1686, was probably O. S., and should now be
reckoned 1687, as the old method of dating was used in
other cases by the clerk that made the record." She also
says: "There is a deed on record from Thomas Holmes
to his son John, of a piece of land in 1709, but I have
found nothing further respecting him." He probably
removed with his son John to East Haddam, in the
Spring of 1714.

Note 4. LONDON, on the river Thames, in England,
"the metropolis of the British empire, and most popu-
lous, wealthy, and commercial city in the world."

Note 5. Counsellor at Law.

Note 6. "*Inns of court,* colleges of common law in
England, in which students have lodgings:—the four
law societies of the Middle Temple, Inner Temple
(formerly belonging to the Knights Templars), Lincoln's
Inn, and Gray's Inn (anciently belonging to the earls

of Lincoln and Gray), which possess the exclusive privi-
lege of conferring the degree of *barrister of law*."

Johnson, Whishaw, quoted by Worcester.

" The Inns of Court, Inner Temple, Middle Temple,
Lincoln's Inn, and Gray's Inn, were originally law colleges, but now only residences for lawyers."

Geographical Dictionary of the British Empire, by James Bryce, Jr.

" The Inns of Court are, the Inner and Middle Temple, Lincoln's Inn, and Gray's Inn ; and there are nine
others of minor character, denominated Inns of Chan-
cery. Each of these is composed of large houses,
surrounding squares, and divided into sets of chambers,
inhabited by barristers, students, attorneys, and soli-
citors."

Thomson's New Universal Gazetteer, 1851, p. 604.

" To Lincoln's Inn are attached Furnival's Inn, on
north side of Holborn, and Thavie's Inn, nearly opposite on south side."

" To Gray's Inn are attached Staple Inn, near Holborn Bars, and Barnard's Inn, in Holborn adjoining
Fetter Lane."

" Gray's Inn derives its name from Edward Lord
Gray of Wilton, who in 1505, sold the manor of Port-
poole, four messuages, four gardens, and other premises
and grounds to Hugh Denny, Esq., from whom they
passed into the possession of the prior and convent of
East Sheen in Surrey, by whom they were leased to certain
students of the Law. The Hall was completed in 1560.

It is a handsome apartment, little inferior to the Middle Temple Hall."

English Cyclopædia, vol. iii., of Geography, p. 594.

"Gray's Inn, north side of Holborn, bequeathed to some students of the law, temp. Edward III, by one of the family of Lords Gray of Wilton. In the hall is a curiously carved oak screen, and some portraits. The garden is spacious, and a great ornament."

Compendious Account of the Counties of England, by Samuel Tymms, vol. vii., p. 30.

Note 7. In the *New England Historical and Genealogical Register*, Vol. X. p. 242, is a very imperfect copy of this *Letter of Directions*, in which this is erroneously called "Saintlands parrish," while in a manuscript copy which came into my hands with the original, it is called "Joint Lands parish," but in the original it is plainly written "Saint-Tandrs-parrich," which is phonetically equivalent to *St. Andrew's parish*, in which stands Gray's Inn, from which, about one fourth of a mile east, stands the church of St. Andrew, on the south side of Holborn, near the foot of the hill, the first building west of Shoe Lane, and nearly opposite Ely Place.

The church was "erected in 1687, under the direction of Sir Christopher Wren; 105 feet in length, 63 in breadth, and 43 in height; the tower is 110 feet high, and was not completed till 1704; the altar-piece and roof are richly ornamented."

Compendious Account, vol. vii., p. 60.

The church built in 1687, was to replace one built at

a much earlier date, as in the time of Henry VII, the rector was fined 4*d.* by the churchwardens, for driving a cart across the church-yard to the rectory; and on a map of London, published in the time of Queen Elizabeth, appears a representation of St. Andrew's church, on the same ground now occupied by the more modern building.

Note 8. HOLBORN is a district in London, containing an area of 196 acres, with a population in 1841, of 39,720, in 1851, of 46,621, and in 1861, of 44,861.

The principal street, of the same name, is about three fourths of a mile long, and lies about half a mile north of, and nearly parallel with, the Thames, and extends nearly due west from Victoria Street to Oxford Street, passing over a steep hill, called Holborn Hill. The name Holborn is derived from a stream called the Old-bourn, which formerly ran there.

"The Olborn, or Holborn, which arose where Middle-row now stands, and flowed down the hill, also fell into Fleet-ditch; and a few houses on its banks were called a village, and distinguished (as early as 1086) by the name of this rivulet."

Picture of London, for 1814, p. 15.

Note 9. In the *Genealogical Register* this is called "Keeper Crown Corte," and in the manuscript copy, "Kasen Crown Court," but the original has it "Rofon Crown Cort," and John Holmes, not being familiar with the localities named, nor with the proper way of spelling their names, took his own way to represent, as well as he could, the names as pronounced by his aged father, who undoubtedly meant in this case the Rose and Crown Court. Perhaps one of the open squares or courts within the Gray's Inn premises, was then known by that name, taking it from some business sign of the Rose and Crown.

Note. 10. Gray's Inn Lane, which runs north from Holborn to the New Road, passing on the east side of Gray's Inn, from which it takes its name, is part of the chief north line of streets which connects the city of London with its northern suburbs.—" On leaving the city walls, the buildings were even less extensive; for, though the *village* of Holborn joined London, the backs of its houses, particularly on the north side, opened into gardens and fields ; a part of Gray's Inn Lane included the only houses that extended out of the main street; the greater part of High Holborn had no existence."—

Historical Illustrations of London, p. 2.

The foregoing description, founded on the map of 1560, was probably not greatly out of the way in 1665, not much new ground having been covered with buildings, as the policy of the government, from 1580, to 1674, seems to have been to prevent the increase of London, (see Note 30) several proclamations and orders in council, for that purpose, having been issued during the several reigns.

Note 11. Upper side is probably intended here, though the words " upper fite" are plainly written, but directly after the word " fite" is an erasure and blotted spot, as if the syllable de had been written after "fite" and then erased.

Note 12. It is difficult for one personally unacquainted in London to fix upon the exact spot indicated in this *Letter of Directions*, as the maps do not now show any "Gray's Inn Walks," which were probably within the grounds of Gray's Inn.

Note 13. The surname THETFORD does not appear in Lower's *English Surnames*, nor in Savage's *Genealogical Dictionary of New England*.

It is evidently one of that class of local surnames which point to the estate or abode of the original assumer, and which are generally derived from cities and towns. It is derived from the ancient town of Thetford, on the south border of the county of Norfolk, eighty miles north-easterly from London, and about thirty-three miles south-east from Lynn, in the same county, which seems once to have been the home of the family of Thomas Holmes.

Thetford lies on both sides of the river Ouse, at the mouth of the river Thet, from which it is named, it being the ford at the Thet, or the Thet ford. It is a very old town, having been the winter quarters of the Danes, in the year 870, and was burned by the Danes in the year 1010.

Note 14. It is not likely that we shall ever know whether Thomas Holmes lost his life while fighting for the King, or for the Parliament, but the time was probably in 1646, when Oxford was besieged by the

Parliamentarians from May 2, till June 24, when, with other places held by the King's forces, it was surrendered by the King's command, which ended the civil war.

Two efforts at besieging the town had been made in the same war, first in 1644, when "Oxford being nearly surrounded by two Parliamentarian armies under the Earl of Essex and Sir William Waller, who intended to besiege it, the King, on the night of June 3, effected his escape from thence, and proceeded to Worcester, on which the Parliamentarians abandoned their intention of siege."

Again, in 1645, when "Oxford was left by the King on May 7, and besieged by General Fairfax, May 22; but the siege raised June 5."

Compendious Account, vol. iv., p. 158.

Note 15. By describing the family coat-of-arms, he evidently intended to help his son to identify the family to which they belonged, which we are unable to do, as a careful search among books upon English Heraldry fails to disclose any such triangular cockfight as he claimed for the family cognizance. James I, referring to the Inns-of-court, ordered that none should be admitted "into the society of any inn, that is not a gentleman by descent," hence, the fact that Thomas Holmes was a member of Gray's Inn, is good evidence that he came within this rule.

"A gentleman, in English Heraldry, taking the largest definition, is a man whose ancestors at a certain time used coats-of-arms, and had a certain rank. This gentility of birth being inheritable may descend to a person of any rank; the proof of the pedigree being all sufficient. Of late years, the rule has fallen into neglect, and probably not one quarter of the Englishmen who style themselves gentlemen and use armorial bearings, could establish their rights."

The Cavalier Dismounted, p. 45.

The necessities of a new country, where enclosures were limited and most of the live stock was pastured on the common or unenclosed lands, led to the adoption of a system which is sometimes called "Yankee Heraldry" under which, as a substitute for the coat-of-arms, John Holmes, the writer of the *Letter of Directions*, chose a "Mark" which was recorded in the *Proprietors*

Book of East Haddam, as follows :— "John holmes his marke for his Creturs is two flits one ye top of ye off eare and a half peny one ye under fide of y^t neare eare. Apriell ye 17th: 1716."

As American Genealogies are so often embellished with cuts of the coats-of-arms to which the families are (or wish they were) entitled, I trust I may be pardoned for giving a representation of the *substitute*, which the descendants of John Holmes may use without fear of having their right questioned by any Heralds College in the world.

Note 16. From this we learn very nearly the time of his emigration, as the "Great Plague" ravaged London in 1665, or from the winter of 1664, till February, 1666. London had often suffered severely from the plague, but never to such an extent as in this last visitation.

From Tymms's *Compendious Account*, vol. 7, pp. 75–89, we extract the following memoranda of the various plague years:

A. D.

" 644. London ravaged by a plague."

" 1349. 50,000 people buried of the plague on the site of the present Charter-house, which was purchased for that purpose. Of this plague, which is thought to have originated in India, Stowe says it so wasted and spoiled the people of England, that scarce the tenth person of all sorts was left alive. The pestilence did not subside till nearly ten years after."

" 1369. This was also a plague year."

" 1407. A plague carried off 30,000 inhabitants."

" 1499–1500. The plague carried off upwards of 30,000 citizens."

" 1513. A plague year."

" 1525. A plague year."

" 1548. A plague year."

" 1563–4. 20,000 persons died of the plague." [In record of " Burials in St. Andrew's Parish, Holborn, Farringdon Ward Without," appear the following entries: " 1563, July 23, Here began the great plague." " 1563–4, — Feb. Here, by God's mercy, the great plague did cease ; whereof died in this parish, this year, to the number of 400, four score and ten." Londinium Redivivum, or an Ancient History and Modern description of London, &c., by James Peller Malcolm, London, 1803, vol. II, p. 221.]

A. D.

" 1574. A plague year."

" 1582. Nearly 7,000 died of the plague."

" 1592. More than 11,000 persons died of the plague."

" 1603. Between 30 and 40,000 persons died of the plague."

" 1625. The plague carried off upwards of 35,000 persons."

" 1636. The plague carried off 11,000 persons."

" 1664-6. This was the period of the great plague, which began at the top of Drury Lane in the winter of 1664, and continued to ravage London with unparalleled severity till February, 1666. It was at its height in September, 1665, when as many as 12,000 persons died in one week, and of them, 4,000 in one night. Defoe, the interesting historian of this awful visitation, declares that 100,000 persons perished. It was, at the commencement, the general opinion of the people that to resist it was to insult the Deity; and at the end it was thought that all would die, and therefore it was not to be shunned. Fires were burnt in the streets to purify the air, but the rain put them out. It ceased in the beginning of the year 1666."

Although Defoe estimated the number of deaths in London, during the great plague, at not less than one hundred thousand, and the official reports show the number of burials to have been 68,596, which was probably far below the real number, yet Appleton's *New*

American Cyclopædia says "it carried off nearly 20,000 persons, or ⅛ of the population," a number so very small as to lead to the supposition that the compiler took it by mistake from the account of that visitation of the plague which occurred one hundred years earlier.

Note 17. " NORFOLK, an extensive county of England, on the eastern coast, bounded N. and N. E. by the German ocean, S. and S. E. by Suffolk, and W. by Cambridgeshire, part of Lincoln, and the Washes. It is almost entirely insulated by the sea, and the rivers which divide it internally from the adjacent counties."

Thomson's New Universal Gazetteer.

Note 18. LYNN REGIS, or KING'S LYNN, is a borough, seaport, and market-town in the county of Norfolk, on the river Ouse, ten miles from its mouth, and ninety-six miles N. E. from London. Four rivulets run through the town, over which are eleven small bridges. On the land side the town is wholly surrounded with a deep wet ditch, flanked by a wall formerly defended by nine bastions, but now much dilapidated. The population in 1851, was 15,751, and in 1861, 16,602.

Thomson's New Universal Gazetteer.

Note 19. It seems probable that the ancestors of Thomas Holmes had lived at Lynn, and this " Small pece of Land" may have been the remnant of a larger estate. Many families in America have been led to expend large sums of money, in a vain search after great estates in England, who could not show by one tenth of the evidence here given, that their ancestors ever had an estate there, of any kind, and some of whom could not even show who were their ancestors. The descendants of Thomas Holmes may be thankful that none of the next-of-kin offices have led them on such a wild-goose-chase.

Note 20. In the *Genealogical Register* this name is called "Edmund But," and in the manuscript copy, before quoted, it is called "Edmund Bool," but in the original it is plainly written Edmond Beel. It is hoped that his descendants still enjoy the use of the "Small pece of Land," and that they are able and willing to account for the unpaid rents for two hundred years.

Note 21. Thomas Holmes probably left London in June, or July, 1665, and he had good cause for thanksgiving that his escape was not cut off by sea, as well as by land.

The following account of the "great plague," taken from the *Encyclopædia Britannica*, eighth edition, vol. 5, pp. 423-4, will show to what degree the fear of infection led the people of the country to shun those from the city.

"In the winter of 1664, two or three isolated cases of plague had occurred in the outskirts of the metropolis, and excited general alarm ; but it was not till about the end of May 1665, that, under the malignant influence of excessive heat, and a close, stagnant atmosphere, the evil burst forth in all its terrors. From the centre of St. Giles the infection spread with rapidity over the adjacent parishes, threatened the court at Whitehall, and, in spite of every precaution crept into the city. A general panic ensued. The nobility and gentry fled ; the royal family followed ; and all who had the power or the means prepared to imitate their example. By every outlet the tide of emigration flowed towards the country, till it was checked by the lord mayor refusing to grant certificates of health, and by the opposition of the neighbouring townships, which rose in their own defence, and drove back the fugitives into the devoted city. The absence of the wealthier class of citizens, and the consequent breaking up of establishments, with the cessation of trade, served to aggravate the calamity ; and although the charity of the opulent seemed to keep pace with the progress of the pestilence, forty thousand servants were left without a home, and the number of artizans and labourers thrown out of employment was still more considerable. The mortality was at first confined to the lower classes, carrying off a larger proportion of children than of adults, and of females than males; but, by the end of June, its diffusion became so rapid, its virulence so great, and its ravages so destructive, that the civil authorities, in virtue of the powers with which they had been invested by an act of James I, 'for the charitable relief and ordering of persons infected with the plague,' divided the parishes into districts, allotting to each a competent number of officers ; and ordered a red cross, one foot in length, to be painted on the door of every infected house, with the words 'Lord have mercy on us,' placed above it, that the healthy might be warned of the existence of the disease. Provision was also made for the interment of the dead. In the day-time persons were always on the watch to withdraw from public view the bodies of those who expired in the street; during the night the tinkling of a bell, accompanied with the lurid glare of torches, announced the approach of the pest-cart making its melancholy round to receive the victims of the previous twenty-four hours. ' No coffins were prepared; no funeral service was read; no mourners were permitted to follow the remains of their relatives and friends. The cart proceeded to the nearest cemetery, and shot its burden into the common grave, a deep and spacious pit, capable of holding some scores of bodies, and dug in the church-yard, or, when the church-yard was full, in the outskirts of the parish.'"

"The distemper generally manifested itself by the febrile symptoms of shivering, nausea, headache, and delirium; but in some these affections were so mild as to be mistaken for a slight and transient indisposition. The insidious approaches of the mortal foe were not discovered, and the patient applied to his usual avocations, till suddenly faintness seized him, the fatal 'tokens' or plague-spots appeared on his breast, and then his hour was come. In most cases, however, the pain and delirium left no room for doubt. The sufferings of the patients were dreadful, and often threw them into paroxysms of frenzy, during which they burst the bands that confined them to their beds, precipitated themselves from the windows, ran naked into the street, and plunged into the river. If the patient survived till the third or fourth day, buboes appeared, and when these could be made to suppurate, recovery might be anticipated; but if the efforts of nature and the physician proved unavailing, death became inevitable. Men of the strongest minds were lost in amazement when they contemplated the woe and desolation wrought by the pestilence; the timid and credulous became the dupes of their own imaginations and the victims of their own terrors; whilst fanaticism scattered abroad its wild predictions and fierce denunciations to add to the inexpressible horror of the scene. During the months of July and August, when the weather was sultry and the heat oppressive, the eastern parishes, which had at first been spared, became the chief seat of the pestilence, and the substantial citizens suffered in common with their poorer neighbours. The regulations of the magistrates could now no longer be enforced. The nights were insufficient for the burial of the dead; coffins were borne along the street at all hours of the day; and the poor burst from their infected dwellings to seek relief for their families, who were perishing of famine as well as of the pestilence. 'London,' says Dr. Lingard, in a passage worthy of Thucydides, 'presented a wide and heart-rending scene of misery and desolation. Rows of houses stood tenantless and open to the winds; others, in almost equal numbers, exhibited the red cross flaming on the doors. The chief thoroughfares, so lately trodden by the feet of thousands, were overgrown with grass. The few individuals who ventured abroad walked in the middle, and, when they met, declined on opposite sides, to avoid the contact of each other. But if the solitude and stillness of the streets impressed the mind with awe, there was something yet more appalling in the sounds which occasionally burst upon the ear. At one moment were heard the ravings of delirium or the wail of woe from the infected dwelling; at another the merry song or the loud and careless laugh from the wassailers at the tavern or the inmates of the brothel. Men became so familiarized with the form, that they steeled their feelings against the terrors of death. They waited each for his turn with the resignation of the Christian or the indifference of the stoic. Some devoted themselves to the exercises of piety, others sought relief in the riot of dissipation or the recklessness of despair.'"

"In September the heat of the atmosphere abated; but, contrary to expectation, the mortality increased. From this time infection became the certain harbinger of death, which followed often within the space of twenty-four hours, generally in the course of three days. An experiment, grounded on the practice of former times, was now ordered to be tried. Fires of sea-coal, in the proportion of one to every twelve houses, were kindled in the streets, courts, and alleys of London and Westminster, and were kept burning three days and nights, till a heavy, continuous rain extinguished them. By the supposed disinfecting power of heat, it was hoped to dissipate the pestilential miasm, or at least to abate its virulence; and in fact, the next report exhibited a considerable diminution in the number of deaths. But whilst the survivors were congratulating themselves on the prospect of deliverance, the destroying angel was scattering a fiercer pestilence from his wings. In the following week, ten thousand victims sank under the accumulated virulence of the disease, and despair reigned in every heart. Yet even now, in this lowest depth of human misery, deliverance was at hand. The high winds which usually accompany the autumnal equinox cooled and purified the air; the weekly number of deaths successively decreased; in the beginning of December seventy-three parishes were pronounced clear of the disease; and in February the court, attended by the nobility and gentry, returned to Whitehall. Upwards of a hundred thousand individuals are said to have perished in London alone; and as the pestilence extended its destructive sway over the greater part of the kingdom, the fugitives from the metropolis carrying the infection with them wherever they found an asylum, the total amount of its ravages must have been truly dreadful."

Note 22. The copy in the *Genealogical Register* says, "wherefore he came here unawares," but the writer of the manuscript copy before noticed, made better sense, and came nearer the true reading of the original in saying "where upon he came for America." It is not strange that they should mistake the word, as it is an original way of spelling Virginia, and is obscurely written.

Note 23. While our sympathy is excited by his inability to return to London as he expected to do, we cannot help thinking that he would have felt as little at home there, two years after he left, as he did in the wilds of Virginia. Nothing in his death-bed story to his son shows that he left any of his kindred living in London, and many of his friends and acquaintances must have died of the plague, while others were driven away; besides which, the appearance of a large part of the city was totally changed by the great fire which happened in the year after he left, beginning on Sunday, Sept. 2,

1666, and "which lasted four days and nights, and destroyed nearly the whole city."

"Londons *Confumption by* Fire."

" Upon the fecond of September 1666, the Fire began in *London* at one *Farryners* Houfe, a Baker, in *Pudding Lane*, between the hours of one and two in the morning, and continued burning until the fixth of *September* following; confuming as by the Surveyors appears in print, three hundred feventy three Acres within the Walls of the City of *London*, and fixty three Acres three Roods without the Walls. There remains feventy five Acres three Roods yet ftanding within the Walls unburnt. Eighty nine Parifh Churches, befides Chappels burnt. Eleven Parifhes within the Walls yet ftanding. Houfes burnt, thirteen thoufand two hundred.

" Per { Jonas Moore
Ralph Gatrix } Surveyors."

The above extract is from a scarce pamphlet of 35 pages, small quarto, entitled

"A True and Faithful

ACCOUNT

OF THE SEVERAL

INFORMATIONS

EXHIBITED

To the Honourable Committee appointed
by the

PARLIAMENT

To Inquire into the late Dreadful Burning
Of the

City of London.

TOGETHER

With other INFORMATIONS touching the
Infolency of POPISH PRIESTS and JE-
SUITES; and the INCREASE of PO-
PERY, brought to the Honourable Committee
appointed by the Parliament for that purpose.

Printed in the Year 1667."

This pamphlet, the object of which was to throw the
responsibility of the fire upon the papists, was reprinted
in 1689, with additions and a different title. "London's Flames Reviv'd: or an Account," &c. I am in-
debted to Mr. Francis S. Hoffman, of New York, for
the loan of these pamphlets from his library, as well as
for other favors of the same nature.

" An Historical Narrative of the Great and Terrible Fire of London, Sept. 2nd 1666," by an anonymous writer, was reprinted by Henry G. Bohn, with the fifth volume of Defoe's works, from which the following is extracted :

" After all examinations there was but one man tried for being the incendiary, who confessing the fact, was executed for it : this was Robert Hubert, a French Hugenot, of Rohan, in Normandy, a person falsely said to be a Papist, but really a sort of lunatic, who by mere accident was brought into England just before the breaking out of the fire, but not landed till two days after, as appeared by the evidence of Laurence Peterson, the master of the ship who had him on board."

" It was soon after complained of, that Hubert was not sufficiently examined who set him to work, and who joined with him. And Mr. Hawles, in his remarks upon Fitzharris's trial, is bold to say that the Commons resolving to examine Hubert upon that matter next day, Hubert was hanged before the house sat, so could tell no farther tales."

" Whatever the unfortunate citizens of London suffered by this dreadful fire, it is manifest, that a greater blessing could not have happened for the good of posterity ; for, instead of very narrow, crooked, and incommodious streets, dark, irregular and ill-contrived wooden houses, with their several stories jutting out, or hanging over each other, whereby the circulation of the air was obstructed, noisome vapours harboured, and verminious, pestilential atoms nourished, as is manifest, by the city not being clear of the plague for twenty-five years before, and only free from contagion three years in above seventy ; enlarging of the streets, and modern way of building, there is such a free circulation of sweet air through the streets, that offensive vapours are expelled, and the city freed from pestilential symptoms : so it may now justly be averred that there is no place in the kingdom where the inhabitants enjoy a better state of health, or live to a greater age, than the citizens of London."

Note 24. It would be very pleasant to trace his wanderings during the interval between his landing in Virginia, and his marriage in New York, and gladly, too, would we learn the exact date of this marriage, which, very likely, was as many as fifteen years after he left London. From the record of baptisms in the Dutch Church in New York, as copied in Valentine's *Manual*, for 1863, it appears that a Thomas Holmes had a son " GRAVO, " baptized there Feb. 10, 1681, but if he were our Thomas Holmes, the son died young, or at least, before his father, as John Holmes was the only child who survived him.

Note 25. The words *after* and *daughter*, were, "in the olden time," very commonly pronounced alike, thus, *arter*, *darter*, so in writing the words, the same rule was applied, and as *arter* was written a f t e r, many persons wrote *darter* d a f t e r. The same rule was applied still further, so that the name *Arthur* is sometimes found on the old records, written A r t e r, and A f t e r.

Note 26. Two Genealogies of the Dudleys have been

published in America; first, *The Dudley Genealogies*, by Dean Dudley, 1848; second, *The Sutton-Dudleys of England, and the Dudleys of Massachusetts*, by George Adlard, 1862; but in neither of them do I find any clue to the family of this Thomas Dodley, or Dudley, as the family tradition calls the name. Perhaps he did not come to America.

Note 27. *Kept,* is probably the word which he intended to write, as Thomas Holmes was then "a very aged man," and, if his father-in-law remained in England, he had long since ceased to keep the tennis-court in London.

Note 28. In the *Genealogical Register* this is called "the laws court," and in the manuscript copy, already mentioned, it is called "the lands court," but both are incorrect. The original is somewhat obscure, as one of the letters, a, is blotted as if it had been written over another to correct it, but all of the other letters are tolerably plain, and nothing can be made of it but "the tanes cort," which was undoubtedly intended for *the tennis-court.*

"TENNIS, a game in which a ball is driven to and fro, by several persons striking it alternately, either with the palm of the hand, naked, or covered with a thick glove, or with a small bat, called a *racket,* held in the hand, the aim being to keep the ball in motion as long as possible without allowing it to fall to the ground."

"*Tennis-courts* were divided by a line stretched in the middle, and the players, standing on each side with their rackets in their hands, were required to strike the ball over this line."

Penny Cyclopædia, quoted by Worcester.

The fact that Thomas Dudley kept the tennis-court in Clare Street, two hundred years ago, will probably help very little in identifying him at this time.

Note 29. This, though plainly written " Clare Streat," is changed to " Clans Street," in the *Genealogical Register*.
Clare Street, in London, lies nearly midway between Covent Garden Market, and Lincoln's Inn Fields ; it is very short, probably not more than one hundred yards in length, extending only from Portugal Street, or Clare Market, to Stanhope Street, crossing which, the street extends, under the name of Blackmore Street, the length of one square, to Drury Lane. Covent Garden, on the other side, as shown in Note 30, formerly came *to* Drury Lane, so it seems that his location of the tennis-court in "Clare Streat in Common Gardin," may not have been very far wrong, though Covent Garden never included the ground now covered by Clare Street.

Note 30. By "Common Gardin in London," he intended Covent Garden, which "was formerly an extensive garden belonging to the Abbot and Convent of Westminster, and thence named *Convent Garden*. It was granted by Edward VI. to the ill-fated Edward Seymour, Duke of Somerset, on whose attainder it was granted to the Russells Earls of Bedford, who built a house for a town residence near the bottom of what is now Southampton Street."

Compendious Account, vol. vii., p. 141.

In the time of Queen Elizabeth, "*Covent Garden,*
literally such, and so called because it belonged to the
Convent at Westminster, extended to St. Martin's Lane,
and the fields behind it reached to St. Giles's. That
lane had few edifices besides the church [St. Martin's-
in-the-Fields]; for Covent Garden wall was on one
side, and a wall which enclosed the King's mews on the
other; and all the upper part was a lane between two
hedges, which extended a little to the west of the village
of St. Giles's."

Historical Illustrations of London, p. 2.

" Leicester-square was all open fields; and St. Mar-
tins-lane had only a few buildings above the church [St.
Martins-in-the-Fields] towards the Convent-garden,
which extended as a garden to Drury-lane, three buildings alone existing in that extensive site."

Leigh's New Picture of London, 1839, p. 12.

The above descriptions are founded on the first map
of London that was ever published, viz: in 1560, in
the third year of Queen Elizabeth.

" Looking at the present extent of London, it is
curious to observe how much anxiety was exhibited in
this reign to prevent the increase of buildings and the
inconvenience of a too-extensive population. By a de-
cree dated Nonesuch, 7th July, 1580, it was forbidden
to erect new buildings where none had before existed in
the memory of man. The extension of the metropolis
was deemed calculated 'to encourage the increase of the
plague; created a trouble in governing such multitudes;
a dearth of victuals; multiplying of beggars, and ina-

bility to relieve them; an increase of artisans more than could live together; impoverishing of other cities for lack of inhabitants. It made lack of air, lack of room to walk, to shoot, &c. And increase of people to rob the queen's customs.' Such were the heads of the lord-treasurer's speech. A proclamation was also issued to the same effect by James I."

Leigh's New Picture of London, 1839, pp. 10–11.

" While the civil wars lasted, little new building was undertaken; but under the Commonwealth it again advanced with rapidity, and, strange to say, a similar proclamation to those of Elizabeth, James, and Charles, was, with certain exceptions, made to impede it. Some of these exceptions were the building of the present Covent-garden by the Earl of Bedford, as also the building of Long-acre, Lincoln's-inn-fields, and Clare-market.

Ibid., p. 14.

Note 31. Our thanks would have been freely given to Mr. Holmes if he had given us a more full account of the family of his mother, and very gladly would we learn the names of her two brothers, and whether they came to America with her, or not, but let us be glad that his descendants have no part in the common tradition, told by so many people, of their descent from "three brothers who came over together," and who generally lost sight of each other directly after landing.

Note 32. " The summer of 1689 was noted for extreme heat; this was followed by a virulent epidemic, which visited almost every family, either in a qualified or mortal form, and proved fatal in more than twenty cases. Most of these occurred in July and August. Mr. Wetherell, then the recorder, inserted in the town book a list of the dead, under the following caption :

"'An account of several persons deceased by the present distemper of sore throat and fever, which distemper hath passed through most families, and proved very mortal with many, especially to those who now have it in this more than ordinary extremity of hot weather, the like having not been known in the memory of man.'"

"Those who perished by this epidemic, above the age of childhood, were Philip Bill, senior; Walter Bodington; Edward Smith and his wife, and their son, John, fifteen years of age; Widow Nicholls, and the wives of Ensign Morgan, Samuel Fox, John Picket, and Mr. Holmes."

History of New London, Conn., by Miss Frances M. Caulkins, p. 198.

In a manuscript letter, dated New London, Conn., Oct. 4, 1860, Miss Caulkins says : " In a list of deaths from an epidemic disorder that prevailed in the summer and autumn of 1689, is the following—July 5, 'The wife of Homes the brick maker Dyed.' There can be little doubt but that this was the wife of *Thomas* Holmes, as no other person of the name appears among the early settlers of the town."

Note 33. "Thomas Holmes Senr of East Haddam, Departted this Life on y^e : 12th Day of December in y^e

year: 1723—in y^e: = 98 — year of his age and the first person in y^e beuriing place where he Was Laid.

And Capt. John Holmes of s^d Haddam, y^e Son of s^d Thomas Holmes, Departed this Life on y^e 29th Day of May in y^e year: 1734 = in y^e: 49 : year of his age.''

Town Records of East Haddam, vol. ii., p. 1117.

This was in the second burial ground in East Haddam, which was laid out in the north part of Hadlyme parish, Dec. 9, 1723, by Joshua Brainerd and Isaac Spencer, town committee, '' near or Joyning to Joseph Dutton's house Lot on the west side of said lot near the upper end.'' It was then by the side of the highway, which was long since discontinued, a new one being laid nearly a quarter of a mile from the burial ground, which is left in the open pasture field, and for nearly forty years no one has been buried there.

Although the *Town Record* says that Thomas Holmes was the first person buried in that yard, a grave stone there, records the death in '' June — 1718,'' of Eliakim Selden, son of Joseph Selden, and tradition says that the first body buried there, was one which the people had started to carry to the burial ground near the Salmon River Cove, but being overtaken by a storm, stopped and buried near the roadside, and this was, perhaps, the reason why the ground was afterwards selected for a public burial place. Thomas Holmes was the first person buried there after the ground was laid out for public use, his death being only three days after it was laid out.

The inscriptions at his grave, though roughly cut with

a pick, on common field stones, are still legible, as
follows :

Head stone.	Foot stone.
Thomas	T—H
Holmes	D—D y^t
D—D	12, 1723.
ye 12—1723	
Age—98.	

Note 34 Dr. Savage, in his *Genealogical Dictionary of
New England*, expresses a doubt as to the age of
Thomas Holmes being so great as 98 years, as recorded
at his grave, and on the town records. A writing, which
I have seen, made as late as 1780, and evidently compiled
mainly from the *Letter of Directions*, says that "he
Came out of England in the time of the Great Plague
—when he was about 17 Years old," but this would
place his birth as late as 1648, which was at least two
years after his father was "Slain att Oxford Sege,"
besides making him only 75 years old at his death,
which would hardly justify the expression that he was
"a very aged man."

Note 35. The expression, "But he is Dead an
Gon and Left but only me his Son" is well calculated
to excite our sympathy for the lonely condition of the
writer, but the effect is somewhat modified by the knowledge that he then had a wife and seven children to
share his grief.

Note 36. John Holmes, as shown in Note 3, was
born March 11, 1686-7, and consequently was thirty-

eight years old in 1725. His mother, as shown in Note 32, died July 5, 1689, which was "6-and thirty year ago" in 1725. The paper referred to in Note 34, says "she Died & Left one Son, which is the above Named John Holmes, at which time he was about Two Years old," thus verifying the supposition of Miss Caulkins as to the style used in recording his birth.

Note 37. From his mode of spelling certain local names it is evident that John Holmes wrote "these directions" from the dictation of his father, but, they could not have been made up in their present form, while his father lived, for they record the fact of his death, and the facts shown in Notes 3, 32, and 36, plainly indicate the summer of 1725, as the time of writing the copy from which we transcribe. This lapse of time between the death of his father and the writing of the *Letter of Directions*, may account for his error in the date of his father's death as shown in Note 33.

The last paragraph was not written by the same hand as the preceding part of the paper, and I am unable to say by whom or at what time it was written, but suppose it was done after the death of John Holmes, in 1734, as an explanation of the history and authority of the document.

GENEALOGY.

EXPLANATION.

THE names of descendants in the male line are arranged in generations, the whole of one generation being given before any of the next; while those in the female line, bearing other names, are given in connection with the names of the parents, in smaller type, and the number of the generation is noted by the small superior figure at the right of the name.

One number, of a regular series, is given to each person named Holmes, for convenient reference, and if that person is named elsewhere, the same number follows his name in brackets, thus [   ], to identify him and refer to his record, but another number following his name in parenthesis, thus (   ), refers to the record of his eldest child.

The Roman numerals before the names of the Holmes descendants, and the Arabic figures before those of other descendants, indicate their order in their respective households.

ABBREVIATIONS.

b.	BORN.	g. dau.	GRANDDAUGHTER.
bap.	BAPTIZED.	m.	MARRIED.
d.	DIED.	unm.	UNMARRIED.
dau.	DAUGHTER.	s. p.	*sine prole*, WITHOUT ISSUE.

When frequently repeated in the same connection, names of towns are represented by their initials.

7

1. THOMAS HOLMES,[1] (2) of whom our only knowledge is gained from the *Letter of Directions*, written by his grandson, m. *Mary Thetford*, and lived in London, England. He was a lawyer, or counsellor, of Gray's Inn, and was killed in the civil war, at the siege of Oxford, probably in May or June, 1646.

Child of THOMAS[1] [1] and MARY (THETFORD) HOLMES.

2. I. THOMAS,[2](3) b. in London, Eng.; thence he came during the "great plague," in 1665, to Virginia, and, after a few years, made his way to New York, where he m. *Lucretia Dudley*, dau. of Thomas Dudley, of London, Eng. They settled in New London, Conn., where she d. July 5, 1689. He removed to East Haddam, with his son John, at whose house he d. Dec. 12, 1723, aged 98 years.

Child of THOMAS[2] [2] and LUCRETIA (DUDLEY) HOLMES.

3. I. JOHN,[3] (4) b. New London, Conn., March 11, 1686-7; m. N. L., Feb. 11, 1706-7, *Mary Willey*, b. N. L., Dec. 10, 1685, dau. of John and Miriam (Moore) Willey. They settled in N. L., where, in 1710, the townsmen leased to him "an acre of rocky land by Cedar Swamp, where his father hath planted some apple trees."

About the spring of 1714, he seems to have removed to " Machamoodus alias East Haddam," where he had bought several parcels of land in Dec. 1713, and Jan. 1713-14. His property was listed at·£46, in 1718, and at £128-18, in 1727. He was Town Surveyor in 1719, and Selectman in 1721.

He d. in East Haddam, May 29, 1734, in the 49th year of his age, according to the town record and the grave stone, but if we have his birth record as it should be, he was in his 48th year.

His widow, Mrs. Mary Holmes, joined the church in E. H., Nov. 3, 1734; and m. (2d) June 1, 1736, Samuel Andrews of E. H., whose first wife, Eleanor Lee, died, leaving him with sixteen children, the youngest less than four years old. Mr. Andrews d. Dec. 14, 1758, but the records do not show the date of her death.

Children of JOHN[3] [3] and MARY (WILLEY) HOLMES.

4. I. THOMAS,[4] (13) b. New London, Conn., Dec. 4, 1707; m. East Haddam, Conn., Jan. 9, 1732, *Lucy Knowlton*, b. E. H., Dec. 11, 1705, dau. of Lieut. Thomas and Susanna Knowlton.

Dec. 4, 1745, he sold his homestead in E. H., to his brother John, and then described himself as " Late of East Haddam In ye County of Hartford, now of Woodbury in the County of Fairfield."

5. II. JOHN,[4] (20) b. N. L., Feb. 24, 1708-9; was bap. and joined the church, E. H., June 8, 1735; he lived in E. H., June 16, 1736, and Aug. 16, 1739; in Saybrook, May 5, 1744; again in E. H.,

Dec. 4, 1745, when he called himself "late of Saybrook," but seems to have again left East Haddam,
for on the 27th of January, 1745–6, he called himself "Late of East Haddam."

He m. *Lucretia Willey*, b. E. H., June 7,
1713, dau. of John and Elizabeth (Harvey) Willey. They lived in Westchester, Conn., May 29,
1748, and a John Holmes, perhaps this one, d. in
that parish, Oct. 12, 1766. A family manuscript,
written as late as 1785, says that they had two sons
and one daughter.

6. III. LUCRETIA,[4] b. N. L., July 14, 1711 ; tradition
says that she m. a man named *Willey*, who d. soon
after marriage, and that she then m. Joseph Willey, b. E. H., Ap. 16, 1705, son of John and
Elizabeth (Harvey) Willey, and it is verified by the
record, which shows that Joseph Willey m. E. H.,
May 22, 1727, Lucretia Willey; from which it appears that she was less than sixteen years old at her
second marriage. The date of her death does not
appear. He had a second wife, Rebecca, by whom
he had nine children. He d. E. H., Jan. 9, 1790.

Children.

1. ELIZABETH,[5] b. E. H., Jan. 24, 1728 ; m. E. H., Sept. 23, 1747,
Samuel Cone, bap. E. H., Sept. 3, 1721, son of Ebenezer Cone, and
g. son of Daniel Cone, one of the original settlers of Haddam. She was
bap. in Hadlyme, May 31, 1752 ; he d. E. H., Ap. 16, 1791, in 70th
year. She d. E. H., Dec. 13, 1814, in 87th year.

Children.

1. *Samuel*,[6] b. E. H., Feb. 20, 1748.
2. *Judah*,[6] b. E. H., July 26, 1753 ; m. E. H., Ap. 10, 1774,
Lydia Cone, b. E. H., Aug. 21, 1754, dau. of Ebenezer and Mary
(Brainerd) Cone. He d. Aug. 13, 1832, aged 79. She d. E. H.,
Oct. 14, 1829, aged 75.

Children.

1. *Clara,*[7] b. E. H., Ap. 1, 1775; m. July 9, 1792, Newton Marsh, son of Edmund and Eleanor[9] [23] (Holmes) Marsh.
2. *Oris,*[7] b. E. H., July 27, 1777; m. Eliphalet Holmes[9] [48].

3. *Joseph Olmsted,*[6] b. E. H., Dec. 19, 1756; was a physician.

2. MARY,[6] b. E. H., Oct. 18, 1730.
3. LUCRETIA,[6] b. E. H., July 9, 1732; m. Feb. 16, 1756, Nathaniel Ackley, b. June 14, 1726, son of Samuel and Bethia Ackley. He d. March 14, 1794, aged 67.
4. JOSEPH,[6] b. E. H., March 22, 1734.
5. ESTHER,[6] b. E. H., May 1, 1736; d. Nov. 13, 1736.
6. BENJAMIN,[6] b. E. H., Sept. 6, 1737.
7. EPHRAIM,[6] b. E. H., July 18, 1740; d. E. H., ——— —, 1816, "aged about 74 years." His wife, Prudence, d. E. H., Ap. 3, 1815, aged 69 years.
8. GRACE,[6] b. E. H., Oct. 6, 1742.

7. IV. MARY,[4] b. N. L., Feb. 7, 1712 [1712–13]; she m. Abel Willey, son of Abel and Hannah (Bray) Willey. They joined the church and she was bap. E. H., June 8, 1735; they removed to Westchester, Conn., where three of their children died during the ministry of Rev. Thomas Skinner, before Dec. 8, 1745. (*N. E. Hist. and Geneal. Register,* viii. 367.) From Westchester they removed to Middle Haddam, Conn., where they joined the church Aug. 2, 1747. The following is probably a very incomplete list of their

Children.

1. JOHN,[5] bap. E. H., Sept. 29, 1735.
2. MARY,[5] bap. Westchester, Ap. 10, 1743.
3. RHODA,[5] bap. Westchester, March 10, 1745.
4. DEBORAH,[5] bap. Middle Haddam, Jan. 25, 1747.

8. V. CHRISTOPHER,[4] (22) b. East Haddam, June 4, 1715; bap. and joined the church E. H., June 8,

1735; m. March 2, 1736, *Sarah Andrews*, b. E. H.,
Feb. 13, 1715–16, bap. July —, 1725, dau. of
Samuel and Eleanor (Lee) Andrews. He was a
constituent member of the church in Hadlyme,
June 26, 1745, and she became a member soon
after. He was chosen Deacon, Jan 18, 1750–51.
She d. Aug. 12, 1782 ; he d. Ap. 12, 1792.

9. VI. Grace,[4] b. E. H., Aug. 4, 1717 ; bap. and
joined the church, E. H., June 8, 1735; m. March
2, 1736, Robert Hungerford, b. E. H., Jan. 3,
1715–16, bap. March 11, 1716, son of John and
Deborah (Spencer) Hungerford. Their names are
on a list of the members of the church in Hadlyme, Sept. 5, 1785. He d. Feb. 11, 1794; she
d. Ap. 27, 1798.

Children.

1. John,[5] b. E. H., Feb. 21, 1736–7 ; m. March 2, 1757, Jane Church of
Lyme. He d. E. H., Dec. 11, 1760.
2. Anna,[5] b. E. H., March 13, 1739 ; d. Jan. 14, 1743–4.
3. Zachariah,[5] b. E. H., March 20, 1741 ; m. Lydia Bigelow. He d.
Nov. 1, 1816, in 76th year; she d. Nov. 14, 1820, ae. 78.
4. Deborah,[5] b. E. H., Oct. 14, 1743 ; m. Uriah Church, bap. E. H., June
15, 1740, son of John and Joanna Church. They settled in Hartland,
where she d. at an advanced age.
5. Silence,[5] b. E. H., May 6, 1747 ; m. Capt. Elnathan Hatch, who was
lost in a brig which he commanded, while on a voyage to the West
Indies. She d. Feb. 7, 1794, (her grave stone erroneously says Feb. 14,)
in 47th year.
6. Anna,[5] b. E. H., Aug. 20, 1749 ; m. Abishai Church, bap. Hadlyme,
May 15, 1748, son of John and Joanna Church. She d. Feb. 24, 1776,
in 27th year.
7. Robert,[5] b. E. H., Jan. 23, 1751–2 ; m. Feb. 14, 1776, Lovice Warner
of Lyme, dau. of Jonathan Warner; she d. May 22, 1777, in 26th year.
He m. (2d) Olive Ely, dau. of Joseph Ely of Lyme. He d. Dec. 29,
1834; she d. July 20, 1843, ae. 85.
8. Grace,[5] b. E. H., Jan. 5, 1755; d. Jan. 15, 1755.
9. Elijah,[5] b. E. H., Nov. 10, 1756; m. Rhoda Harvey, b. E. H., Dec.
4, 1758, dau. of Robert and Rachel Harvey. He d. Dec. 8, 1839; she d.
Jan. 20, 1835.
10. Grace,[5] b. E. H., Aug. 16, 1759 ; d. Nov. 5, 1759.

10. VII. ELIPHALET,[4] (36) b. E. H., July 12, 1722; bap. May 4, 1735; m. Jan. 25, 1742, *Damaris Waterhouse.* He d. Nov. 30, 1743, and his widow m. (2d) Joseph Comstock of E. H., by whom she had five children.

11. VIII. SARAH,[4] b. E. H., June 14, 1726; bap. May 4, 1735; m. *Nathaniel Niles.*

12. IX. ABIGAIL,[4] b. E. H., Aug. 1, 1729; bap. May 4, 1735; was a member of Hadlyme church, Sept. 14, 1785; d. Aug. 26, 1811, unm.

Children of THOMAS[4] [4] and LUCY (KNOWLTON) HOLMES.

13. I. LUCY,[5] b. E. H., Sept. 26, 1733.

14. II. SUSANNA,[5] (twin) b. E. H., May 26, 1735.

15. III. MARY,[5] (twin) b. E. H., May 26, 1735.

16. IV. GRACE,[5] b. E. H., Sept. 26, 1736.

17. V. THOMAS,[5] b. E. H., June 25, 1740.

18. VI. THETFORD,[5] b. E. H., May 17, 1742.

19. VII. ELIPHALET,[5] b. E. H., July 17, 1744.

Children of JOHN[4] [5] and LUCRETIA (WILLEY) HOLMES.

20. I. JOHN,[5] bap. E. H., Sept. 3, 1738.

21. II. JESSE,[5] bap. Westchester, Conn., May 29, 1748, by Rev. Benjamin Bowers, of Middle Haddam.

Children of CHRISTOPHER[4] [8] and SARAH (ANDREWS) HOLMES.

22. I. JOHN,[5] (38) b. E. H., Nov. 18, 1736; bap.
Feb. 6, 1736–7; m. Ap. 22, 1762, *Mercy Canfield*
of Saybrook, Conn. She was bap. in Hadlyme,
May 25, 1766. They settled in E. H., but removed to Campton, N. H., where they died.

23. II. ELEANOR,[5] b. E. H., Aug. 3, 1738; bap. Sept. 24,
1738; m. **Edmund Marsh**, son of John and
Submit (Woodward) Marsh. She d. Oct. 9, 1792,
in 55th year; he d. Dec. 30, 1811, aged 78 years.

Children.

1. EDMUND,[6] settled in New Hampshire.
2. JOHN,[6] settled in New Hampshire.
3. CHRISTOPHER,[6] d. young.
4. WOODWARD,[6] m. Jan. 7, 1788, Mary Cone.
5. SYLVESTER,[6] m. Phebe Brooks, dau. of Samuel and Rhoda Brooks. He
   d. at Kingston, N. Y., June 22, 1794, ae. 26; she d. Hadlyme, Ap. 11,
   1842, ae. 74.

Children.

1. *Phebe*,[7] lives in Hadlyme, 1864.
2. *Nancy*,[7] m. Alfred Dean, La Salle, Ill.
3. *Fanny*,[7] m. Denison Babcock of Hamilton, N. Y., both dead.
4. *Vesta*,[7] m. Warren Fuller, of Olmsted, O.

6. NEWTON,[6] m. July 9, 1792, Clara Cone, b. Ap. 1, 1775, dau. of Judah
   Cone, and great grand daughter of Lucretia Holmes,[4] [6].
7. SARAH,[6] m. Samuel Brooks, Jr.
8. HOLMES,[6] m. Keturah Boon, who d. Jan. 12, 1816, aged 38 years.
9. CHRISTOPHER,[6] m. Ann Mack.
10. A SON,[6] (name not on record) d. Aug. 13, 1786, aged about 7 years.
11. ALICE,[6] d. Ap. 5, 1811, in 31st year.

24. III. CHRISTOPHER,[5] b. E. H., Sept. 17, 1739; bap.
Oct. 21, 1739; d. Nov. 11, 1760.

25. IV. URIEL,[5] (47) b. E. H., June 11, 1741; bap.
July 12, 1741; m. July 1, 1764, *Statira Cone*, b.

8

E. H., July 9, 1749, bap. Millington, Aug. 6, 1749, dau. of Jonah and Elizabeth (Gates) Cone.

They settled in Hartland, Conn., where he was a prominent citizen, being Justice of the Peace, Representative in the Legislature, Deacon of the Church, and Colonel of Militia. He joined the church in Hartland, May 12, 1769; his wife joined same church Sept. 11, 1774. He gave a bell and communion service to the church in 1776, and was chosen Deacon, March 22, 1779. He d. Nov. 7, 1809, according to his grave stone, while the church record says Nov. 6. She d. Dec. 6, 1812.

26. V. SARAH,[5] b. E. H., Dec. 5, 1742; bap. Jan. 30, 1742-3; m. Nov. 17, 1768, Edmund Grindal Rawson, b. —— —, son of Rev. Grindal and Dorothy (Chauncy) Rawson. He graduated at Yale College, 1759; studied theology, and preached occasionally. They settled in Hadlyme, where she d. Ap. 27, 1821; he d. July 21, 1823, ae. 84.

Children.

1. CHARLES CHAUNCY,[6] (twin) b. E. H., July 27, 1769; d. in Bermuda, June 29, 1788, ae. 19.
2. JOHN WILSON,[6] (twin) b. E. H., July 27, 1769; d. —— —, aged 9 years.
3. THOMAS HOOKER,[6] b. E. H., Sept. 24, 1770.
4. EDMUND GRINDAL,[6] b. E. H., Jan. 26, 1772.
5. DOROTHY BLACKLEACH,[6] b. E. H., Oct. 17, 1773; d. Oct. 31, 1774.
6. OZIAS HOLMES,[6] b. E. H., Ap. 22, 1775.
7. JOSEPH PERN,[6] b. E. H., Dec. 23, 1776.
8. SARAH ANDREWS,[6] b. E. H., Dec. 31, 1778; m. Feb. 6, 1803, as a second wife, Oliver Usher, b. Chatham, Conn., Sept. 16, 1766, son of Robert and Susanna (Gates) Usher.
9. DOROTHY NICHOLS,[6] b. E. H., July 16, 1780.
10. AN INFANT,[6] d. E. H., May 9, 1785.
11. CATHERINE CHAUNCY,[6] b. E. H., Feb. 4, 1788; m. Dec. 30, 1812, as a second wife, George Palmer, b. E. H., May 22, 1781, son of Levi and Elizabeth (Cone) Palmer. She d. E. H., May 14, 1826, aged 38 years.

12. CHARLES WILSON,* birth not on record, m. Mary Shackleford of Gwinnett Co., Ga., and d. leaving five children. (*Rawson Memorial*, p. 50.)

27. VI. LUCRETIA,⁵ b. E. H., March 20, 1745; d. Feb. 11, 1760.

28. VII. ELIPHALET,⁵ (48) b. E. H., Feb. 3, 1746-7; bap. Hadlyme, March 22, 1746, O. S.; m. Jan. 8, 1772, *Anne Gates*, b. E. H., March 21, 1750, bap. June 9, 1750, dau. of Joseph and Abigail (Fuller) Gates. She d. Aug. 24, 1828; he d. Feb. 14, 1833.

29. VIII. MEHITABEL,⁵ b. E. H., Oct. 3, 1748; bap. Hadlyme, Nov. 6, 1748; m. Dec. 12, 1770, Mr. James Sparrow of E. H.; he d. Jan. 29, 1774, in 39th year; and she m. (2d) Feb. 28, 1775, Dr. Augustus Mather of Lyme, Conn. He joined the church in Millington, from first church in Lyme, June 29, 1777; she joined same church June 6, 1790, and d. Ap. 16, 1810. He m. (2d) May 8, 1811, Hannah Ransom.* He d. July 5, 1832, in 85th year.

Children.

1. SARAH,⁶ (Sparrow) b. E. H., Sept. 15, 1771.
2. MEHITABEL,⁶ (Mather) b. E. H., Nov. 21, 1775.
3. AUGUSTUS,⁶ b. E. H., Ap. 6, 1778.
4. MARY,⁶ b. E. H., Dec. 21, 1780.
5. JAMES,⁶ b. E. H., Dec. 30, 1783.
6. OZIAS,⁶ b. E. H., Jan. 22, 1787.

30. IX. SAMUEL,⁵ b. E. H., Ap. 11, 1750; bap. Hadlyme, Ap. 15, 1750; m. *Mehitabel Ely* of Lyme,

---

* Dr. Mather, by this second marriage, had one son, Eleazer Watrous Mather, b. E. H., March 28, 1812; bap. Millington, Aug. 30, 1812; m. June 19, 1837, Elizabeth Louisa Foster, and resides at East Haddam.

and removed to Campton, N. H., where they both
d. *s. p.*

31. X. MARY,⁵ b. E. H.. Jan. 9, 1751 ; bap. Hadlyme, Feb. 23, 1752; d. June 25, 1753.

32. XI. MARY,⁵ b. E. H., Feb. 8, 1754; bap. Hadlyme, March 24, 1754; d. Oct. 3, 1754.

33. XII. EBENEZER,⁵ (53) b. E. H., Sept. 24, 1755;
bap. Hadlyme, Nov. 2, 1755 ; m. Sept. 24, 1789,
Abigail Gates, b. Sept. 9, 1760, bap. Oct. 12, 1760,
dau. of Joseph and Abigail (Fuller) Gates. Capt.
Ebenezer Holmes d. Aug. 23, 1833 ; his widow
d. Sept. 29, 1838.

34. XIII. OZIAS,⁵ b. E. H. July 24, 1757; bap. Hadlyme, July 31, 1757; d. Dec. 24, 1776.

35. XIV. CHRISTOPHER,⁵ (59) b. E. H., July 5, 1762;
bap. Hadlyme, Aug. 8, 1762; was a physician,
settled in his native place ; m. March 14, 1793,
Esther Beckwith, b. E. H., Feb. 27, 1776, dau. of
Asa and Abigail (Warner) Beckwith. He. d. Feb.
1, 1812; she was bap. and joined the church in
Hadlyme, May 4, 1828, and d. Jan. 9, 1834.

Children of ELIPHALET⁴ [10] and DAMARIS (WATERHOUSE) HOLMES.

36. I. HULDAH,⁵ b. E. H., Aug. 19, 1743.

37. II. PATIENCE,⁵ b. E. H.,—— ——; bap. Hadlyme, Feb. 23, 1745–6.

Children of JOHN⁵ [22] and MERCY (CANFIELD) HOLMES.

38. I. JOHN,⁶ b. E. H., Feb. 22, 1763; bap. Hadlyme, June 29, 1766; settled at Portland, Me.

39. II. JOEL,⁶ b. E. H., Feb. 5, 1765; bap. Hadlyme, June 29, 1766; d. at Campton, N. H.

40. III. CHAUNCY,⁶ b. E. H., Nov. 15, 1766; bap. Hadlyme, Jan. 4, 1767;* settled in Belfast, Me.

41. IV. MARY,⁶ b. E. H., Sept. 11, 1768; bap. Hadlyme, —— ——, 1768; m. *Nathan Stearns*, and settled near Montreal, Canada East.

42. V. URIEL,⁶ bap. Hadlyme, May 27, 1770; d. soon.

43. VI. URIEL,⁶ b. E. H., Jan. 8, 1772; bap. Hadlyme, March 1, 1772.

44. VII. CHRISTOPHER,⁶ b. E. H., March 30, 1774; bap. Hadlyme, June 19, 1774.

45. VIII. SARAH,⁶ b. —— ——; m. *Samuel Stearns*, a brother of Nathan, and settled near Montreal, C. E.

46. IX. SAMUEL,⁶ (68) b. Campton, N. H., July 14, 1780; another record says, July 23, 1779; m. *Martha Palmer*, b. Campton, Oct. 7, 1780; another record says Oct. 19, 1779, dau. of Joseph and Martha (Taylor) Palmer.† He d. C., Ap. 20, 1838, ae. 58; she d. C., May 30, 1836, ae. 56.

---

* The record of baptism has the date 1766, a mistake very commonly made at the beginning of the year, but the calendar shows that Jan. 4, 1767, was on Sunday, and that was, without doubt, the day of the baptism.
† Martha Taylor was b. Ap. 14, 1763.

Child of URIEL[6] [25] and STATIRA (CONE) HOLMES.

47. I. URIEL,[6] (78) b. E. H., Aug. 26, 1764; bap.
Hartland, June 11, 1769; grad. Yale Col. 1784,
and settled in Litchfield, Conn., as a lawyer, a few
years subsequently. He m. Oct. 24, 1794, *Esther
Austin*, b. New Hartford, May 6, 1772, dau. of
Hon. Aaron and Sarah (Kellogg) Austin of New
Hartford, Conn.; she d. Litchfield, Aug. 30, 1802.
He was elected a Representative in the Conn. Legislature, nine times, was a Judge of the Litchfield
County Court from 1814 to 1817, and during the
latter year he was chosen a Representative in Con-
gress, but resigned in 1818. While passing through
Canton, Conn., he was thrown from his carriage,
and so injured as to cause his death, May 18,
1827, in the 63d year of his age. He was buried
in Litchfield.

Children of ELIPHALET[6] [28] and ANNA (GATES) HOLMES.

48. I. ELIPHALET,[6] (81) b. E. H., Ap. 25, 1776; m.
March 14, 1798, *Oris Cone*, b. E. H., July 27,
1777, dau. of Judah and Lydia (Cone) Cone, and
g. g. dau. of Lucretia,[4] [6]. She was bap. and
joined the church at Hadlyme, June 5, 1808; he
d. Dec. 10, 1857, ae. 82; she d. Ap. 14, 1863,
ae. 86.

49. II. ANNE,[6] b. E. H., Jan. 30, 1781: d. at New
Haven, Conn., Aug. 31, 1795; buried at Hadlyme.

50. III. Lucretia,[6] b. E. H., Sept. 18, 1785; d. Oct. 11, 1791. ~

51. IV. Ozias,[6] (83) b. E. H., Ap. 2, 1789; m. Jan. 19, 1808, *Betsy Tully*, b. March 18, 1787, dau. of Elias and Azubah (Kirtland) Tully. He d. Aug. 26, 1845; she d. Dec. 1, 1855, aged 68 years.

52. V. Joseph,[6] b. E. H., May 13, 1791; d. Oct. 13, 1810, "in the last year of his Collegiate life, much regretted by his Classmates and all of his friends." (Grave stone.)

Children of Ebenezer[6] [33] and Abigail (Gates) Holmes.

53. I. Abigail,[6] b. E. H., July 31, 1792; bap. and joined the church in Hadlyme, June 4, 1815; resides in E. H., with her brother Ebenezer, unm.

54. II. Lucretia,[6] b. E. H., March 2, 1794; bap. and joined the church in Hadlyme, May 1, 1814; m. Aug. 14, 1830, *Daniel Woodworth* of E. H.; this was the last marriage recorded by Rev. Joseph Vaill. She d. at Danielsonville, Conn., Sept. 4, 1852.

55. III. Ebenezer,[6] b. E. H., Aug. 1, 1797; resides in E. H., unm.

56. IV. Nancy,[6] b. E. H., March 11, 1799; bap. and joined the church in Hadlyme, Nov. 18, 1827; resides in New York city, unm.

57. V. A Daughter,[6] b. E. H., Sept. 30, 1801 ; d. Dec. 31, 1801.

58. VI. Noah,[6] b. E. H., May 6, 1803; d. at sea, Ap. 28, 1830, was buried in the Mediterranean.

Children of Christopher[5] [35] and Esther (Beckwith) Holmes.

59. I. Sarah,[6] b. E. H., July 15, 1793; bap. and joined the church in Hadlyme, Aug. 5, 1827; d. March 22, 1863, ae. 70.

60. II. Samuel,[6] (85) b. E. H., July 10, 1795; m. Mrs. *Cornelia* (Luther) *Buckingham*, dau. of Ansel Luther and widow of Aaron Buckingham. He d. Jan. 3, 1852, and she m. (3d) Henry Smith, and removed to South Glastenbury, Conn.

61. III. Esther,[6] b. E. H., Sept. 24, 1797; m. Ap. 8, 1819, Charles Attwood, b. E. H., March 19, 1795, son of Capt. Oliver and Dorothy (Chapman) Attwood. She d. Jan. 17, 1832.

Children.

1. Charles,[7] b. E. H., Feb. 28, 1820; m. Nov. 18, 1846, Martha Thompson Greene, b. Johnsonburg, N. J., Ap. 19, 1826, dau. of Dr. David and Ann Breckenridge (Thompson) Greene; he resides in New York city, a merchant.

Children.

1. *Emma Louise,*[8] b. N. Y., March 4, 1848.
2. *Annie Breckenridge,*[8] b. N. Y., June 30, 1850.
3. *Archibald Finn,*[8] b. N. Y., July 10, 1860; d. May 12, 1861, aged 10 mo. 2 days.
4. *Aline,*[8] b. N. Y., Aug. 7, 1862.

2. OLIVER,[7] b. E. H., July 1, 1821; d. Nov. 19, 1845, aged 24.
3. CHRISTOPHER HOLMES,[7] b. E. H., May 22, 1824.
4. SARAH CATHERINE,[7] b. E. H., July 30, 1826; m. Dec. 10, 1849, Amos Stanton Harvey, b. Colchester, Conn., Jan. 5, 1825, son of Elias and Ruth (Edwards) Harvey. They reside in E. H.

Children.

1. *Kate Russell,*[8] b. E. H., June 11, 1854.
2. *Mary Esther,*[8] b. E. H., Sept. 1, 1862.

5. SAMUEL,[7] b. E. H., June 22, 1828; d. Dec. 21, 1828.
6. MARY ELIZA,[7] b. E. H., Ap. 22, 1830, m. Nov. 27, 1862, Ralph Bliss Swan, b. Ap. 17, 1839, son of Diodate Lord and Mary Eliza (Welles) Swan. They reside in E. H.

62. IV. MARY,[6] b. E. H., May 4, 1800; m. Nov. 29, 1832, Capt. *Charles Attwood,* whose first wife was her sister Esther. She d. May 27, 1837, *s. p.*; and he m. (3d) Dec. 31, 1837, Julia Ann Chapman, b. Dec. 12, 1799, dau. of John and Sarah (Hubbard) Chapman, and now lives in E. H.

63. V. ELIZA,[6] b. E. H., July 14, 1803; bap. and joined church in Hadlyme, Nov. 18, 1827, resides in Hadlyme, unm.

64. VI. CHRISTOPHER COLUMBUS,[6] (88) b. E. H., Aug. 8, 1805; m. March 19, 1837, *Ellen Elizabeth Sellew,* b. Glastenbury, Conn., May 1, 1814, dau. of Russell and Mary (Loveland) Sellew. They reside in Hadlyme.

65. VII. JOHN,[6] (91) b. E. H., Jan. 30, 1808; m. Ap. 26, 1840, *Mariè Antoinette Foster,* b. E. H., "Sunday, Nov. 29, 1818, 9 P. M.," dau. of Nathan Lanesford and Azubah Louisa (Cone) Foster. He d. Hadlyme, Nov. 29, 1856.

9

66. VIII. MEHITABEL,[6] b. E. H., Ap. 20, 1810; bap. and joined the church in Hadlyme, Nov. 18, 1827; resides in Hadlyme, unm.

67. IX. JOSEPH URIEL,[6] b. E. H., July 6, 1812; d. Hadlyme, July 17, 1860, unm.

Children of SAMUEL[6] [46] and MARTHA (PALMER) HOLMES.

68. I. ALMIRA,[7] b. Campton, N. H., May 19, 1803; m. Jan. 31, 1837, Tillotson Pierce, b. July 9, 1797.

Children.

1. A SON,[8] b. Thornton, N. H., Ap. 3, 1838; d. Aug. 2, 1838.
2. JOSEPHINE,[8] b. Thornton, N. H., May 26, 1839.
3. CAROLINE,[8] b. Sandwich, N. H., May 19, 1840.
4. MARTHA JANE,[8] b. S., Aug. 13, 1842.
5. HENRIETTA,[8] b. S., June 26, 1846.

69. II. ELIZA,[7] b. C., Jan. 4, 1805; m. *Daniel James.*

70. III. THIRZA,[7] b. C., Sept. 27, 1806; m. Ap. 4, 1830, Chauncy Beckwith Phelps, b. E. H., June 26, 1802, son of Niles and Esther (Peck) Phelps.* They live in E. H., in Hadlyme society.

Children.

1. A DAUGHTER,[8] b. E. Haddam, Feb. 5, 1831; d. same day.
2. SAMUEL HOLMES,[8] b. E. H., Feb. 3, 1832.
3. ESTHER PECK,[8] b. E. H., March 26, 1833; m. July 23, 1863, Samuel Jones of E. H., b. Chester, Conn., Oct. 25, 1823, son of Ansel and Deborah (Clark) Jones.

Child.

1. *Charles Leslie,*[9] b. E. H., Ap. 7, 1864.

---

* The first wife of Chauncy Beckwith Phelps was Flora Fuller, dau. of William Ward and Susanna (Knowlton) Fuller of E. H.; she d. Nov. 21, 1829, ae. 28; leaving one child, William Fuller Phelps, b. Nov. 5, 1829.

4. MARTHA PALMER,[8] b. E. H., Dec. 8, 1834; m. Aug. 12, 1855, Samuel Wilson Gates, b. E. H., June 12, 1832, son of Samuel and Mary (Stranahan) Gates.

Children.

1. *Albert Wilson*[9] b. E. H., Oct. 8, 1856; d. July 25, 1864.
2. *Charles Wesley,*[9] b. E. H., July 7, 1862; d. Sept. 5, 1862.

5. EDWIN HAYNES,[8] b. E. H., Feb. 21, 1836; m. March 22, 1863, Mrs. Harriet Diantha (Chapman) Gates, b. Middle Haddam, May 23, 1839, dau. of Reuben and Martha (Rich) Chapman, and widow of Frederick William Gates of E. H.
6. JOSEPH PALMER,[8] b. E. H., Ap. 26, 1838; m. July 15, 1860, Harriet Jennet Gates, b. E. H., July 25, 1840, dau. of Samuel and Mary (Stranahan) Gates.
7. MARO,[8] b. E. H., July 1, 1840; m. June 1, 1864, Alice Geer.
8. MARYETTE,[8] b. E. H., Jan. 1, 1843, m. Dec. 14, 1861, Rufus Griswold Phelps, b. May 4, 1833, son of Griswold Comstock and Lydia (Chadwick) Phelps.

Child.

1. *Arthur Lanesford,*[8] b. July 23, 1862.

9. EMILY,[8] b. E. H., July 11, 1845.
10. HARRIET,[8] b. E. H., March 11, 1848.
11. FREEMAN,[8] b. E. H., Jan. 19, 1850.

71. IV. EMILY,[7] b. C., May 12, 1808; d. young.

72. V. OZIAS,[7] b. C., Ap. 2, 1810; m. *Elizabeth Cook;* lives in Campton.

73. VI. JOSEPH,[7] (97) b. C., July 28, 1812; m. *Hannah Bump,* b. Aug. 30, 1820; lives in Campton.

74. VII. CAROLINE,[7] b. C., Nov. 8, 1814; m. *Leonard Foss.*

75. VIII. ELVIRA,[7] b. C., Dec. 7, 1816; m. *George*

Howell, b. E. H., Ap. 29, 1817, son of Daniel Kirtland and Hannah (North) Howell; they live in Hadlyme, *s. p.*

76. IX. ELIZUR,⁷ (105) b. C., Dec. 30, 1818; m. *Martha Blaisdell*, b. March 10, 1827; he d. C., May 15, 1850.

77. X. DRURY,⁷ b. C., June 13, 1822; lives in Hadlyme, unm.

Children of URIEL⁸ [47] and ESTHER (AUSTIN) HOLMES.

78. I. HENRY,⁷ b. Litchfield, Conn., Feb. 14, 1795; grad. M. D. Yale Col. 1825; never married; resides in Hartford, Conn.

79. II. URIEL,⁷ b. L., Sept. 15, 1796; grad. Yale Col. 1816; entered Andover Theological Seminary with the class that graduated in 1820, but died July 4, 1818, having been in the institution less than a year.

80. III. CAROLINE,⁷ b. L., May 12, 1799; d. May 28, 1802.

Children of ELIPHALET⁰ [48] and ORIS (CONE) HOLMES.

81. I. ANNE,⁷ b. E. H., Aug. 11, 1799; bap. Hadlyme, June 5, 1808; joined the church in Hadlyme, Jan. 6, 1828; resides with her brother, unm.

82. II. TIMOTHY,⁷ (107) b. E. H., Feb. 24, 1802;

bap. Hadlyme, June 5, 1808 ; m. May 8, 1826, *Phebe Howell Rose*, b. Bridgehampton, Long Island, Oct. 30, 1800, dau. of Stephen and Phebe (Howell) Rose. They joined the church, and she was bap. in Hadlyme, Jan. 6, 1828. They live in Hadlyme, on the homestead of his grand father, Judah Cone.

Children of OZIAS[6] [51] and BETSEY (TULLY) HOLMES.

83. I. MARY ANN,[7] b. Feb. 4, 1809 ; bap. and joined the church in Hadlyme, Nov. 18, 1827 ; m. Nov. 8, 1829, Joseph Warner, b. Lyme, Conn., Dec. 3, 1792, son of Selden and Dorothy (Selden) Warner; they settled in Lyme, Hadlyme society, where he d. June 13, 1861.

Children.

1. NANCY HOLMES,[8] b. Lyme, Sept. 12, 1830 ; bap. May 29, 1831.
2. ELIZABETH ANN,[8] b. L., March 21, 1834.
3. JOSEPH SELDEN,[8] b. L., Feb. 22, 1837.

84. II. JOSEPH,[7] (108) b. Dec. 17, 1817 ; m. May 21, 1844, *Maria Kirtland Selden*, b. Greenfield, Erie Co., Penn., Ap. 21, 1824, dau. of Joseph and Mary Ann (Kirtland) Selden. She d. Lebanon, Conn., Dec. 30, 1859 ; and he m. (2d) June 19, 1860, Sarah Eliza Morgan, b. Ap. 26, 1838, dau. of Griswold Edwin and Eliza J. (Saxton) Morgan. (See *Morgan Genealogy*, p. 14.) He lives in Lebanon.

Child of SAMUEL[6] [60] and CORNELIA (LUTHER) HOLMES.

85. I. SAMUEL THETFORD.[7]

86. II. THOMAS BENTON.[7]

87. III. MARY ELIZA.[7]

Children of CHRISTOPHER COLUMBUS[6] [64] and ELLEN ELIZABETH (SELLEW) HOLMES.

88. I. ESTHER ELIZABETH,[7] b. Aug. 1, 1839; d. Oct. 20, 1857.

89. II. CHRISTOPHER,[7] b. May 25, 1844.

90. III. CHARLEMAGNE,[7] b. Feb. 1, 1847.

Children of JOHN[6] [65] and MARIÈ ANTOINETTE (FOSTER) HOLMES.

91. I. JOHN,[7] b. Oct. 14, 1841.

92. II. HENRY,[7] b. Dec. 3, 1842.

93. III. REGINALD HEBER,[7] b. Nov. 19, 1845; d. May 31, 1862.

94. IV. WILLIAM CONE,[7] b. Jan. 22, 1848.

95. V. MARY LOUISE,[7] b. Oct. 20, 1851; d. Ap. 4, 1854.

96. VI. CHARLES ATTWOOD,[7] b. Ap. 7, 1855.

Children of JOSEPH[7] [73] and HANNAH (BUMP) HOLMES.

97. I. ORLANDO MARTEL,[8] b. Campton, N. H., March 6, 1842.

98. II. JOHN SOUTHMAYD,[8] b. C., Oct. 2, 1843.

99. III. DRURY ERVIN,[8] b. C., June 24, 1845.

100. IV. JOSEPH ALPHONSO,[8] b. C., Aug. 2, 1847.

101. V. BENJAMIN SOUTHMAYD.[8]

102. VI. JAMES EBER.[8]

103. VII. A DAUGHTER,[8] (twin).

104. VIII. A DAUGHTER,[8] (twin).

Children of ELIZUR[7] [76] and MARTHA (BLAISDELL) HOLMES.

105. I. ALFRED F.,[8] b. Campton, N. H., Ap. 3, 1829.

106. II. ———— ————.[8]

Child of TIMOTHY[7] [82] and PHEBE HOWELL (ROSE) HOLMES.

107. I. SILAS ROSE,[8] (117) b. E. H., Aug. 9, 1827; bap. Hadlyme, Jan. 20, 1828; m. June 9, 1851, *Emily Adeline Rose*, b. New York City, Jan. 31, 1833, dau. of Silas and Eliza (Fordham) Rose. He represented the town of East Haddam, in the Legislature of Conn., in 1861; resides with his father.

Children of JOSEPH[7] [84] and MARIA KIRTLAND (SELDEN) HOLMES.

108. I. MARY SELDEN,[8] b. E. H., Dec. 23, 1846.

109. II. ELIZABETH KIRTLAND,[8] b. E. H., Nov. 19, 1848.

110. III. HARRIET TULLY,[8] b. Colchester, Conn., May 13, 1850.

111. IV. JOSEPHINE,[8] b. Lebanon, Conn., May 31, 1852 ; d. Dec. 26, 1852.

112. V. ADELAIDE MARIA,[8] b. Leb., Sept. 27, 1854.

113. VI. JOSEPH SELDEN,[8] b. Leb., Ap. 19, 1856.

114. VII. CAROLINE,[8] b. Leb., July 13, 1858 ; d. Dec. 16, 1859.

Children of JOSEPH[7] [84] and SARAH ELIZA (MORGAN) HOLMES.

115. VIII. GEORGIANA MORGAN,[8] b. Leb., Aug. 22, 1862 ; d. March 8, 1863.

116. IX. HOWARD,[8] b. Leb., March 15, 1864.

Children of SILAS ROSE[8] [107] and EMILY ADELINE (ROSE) HOLMES.

117. I. ANNIE MARIA,[9] b. E. H., Dec. 19, 1852.

118. II. PHEBE ELIZA,[9] b. E. H., July 5, 1855.

119. III. MARY LUCRETIA,[9] b. E. H., Oct. 28, 1858; d. Ap. 11, 1859.

120. IV. STEPHEN ELIPHALET,[9] b. E. H., Nov. 28 1862.

INDEX.

HOLMES, CHRISTIAN NAMES.

INDEX.

NAMES OTHER THAN HOLMES.

[But one reference is made though a name occurs several times on a page.]

www.ingramcontent.com/pod-product-compliance
Lightning Source LLC
Chambersburg PA
CBHW030009030726
47499CB00008B/2966